ALWAYS TRY JUST ONE MORE TIME
An Inspirational Handbook for Life

DELLA FAYE

KORLOKI PUBLISHING

NEW YORK

ISBN: 978-1936739158
ISBN: 1936739151

Newly Revised Edition
First printing 2005
Second printing 2012

Unless otherwise noted, all Scripture references are from the King James Version (KJV) of the Bible.

ISBN: 978-1936739158 / 1936739151
Always Try Just One More Time / Della Faye

PUBLISHED BY KORLOKI PUBLISHING
www.kpcbooks.com
New York

Printed in the United States of America

DEDICATION

I dedicate this revised edition to my family, and the many friends I have met, people who have inspired me, and those I have encouraged and provided hope over the years.

ACKNOWLEDGEMENTS

Rainey Smith, Andy Linman, and Professor William Matter thanks for proofing the drafts and helping with the corrections for the first printing. Donna Woodruff thanks for encouraging me to write a book. Alice Walker, Linda Hannon, "Pumpkin" McGruder, and Anita Gilyard, thank you for allowing me to share your stories. To Carmen Curry, Walter Thomas, Melissa White, and Diane Garrett, thank you for the mental pushes. Geraldine Robbins, Jacquie Young, and Cheryl Williamson, I'm sure you'll find many people who occasionally wanted to strangle my neck besides you. Family members, friends, and coworkers, thank you for your prayers and for putting up with my strong inner convictions and me.

Almighty God, my Lord and Savior Jesus Christ, and the Holy Spirit thank you for your love, grace, and mercy. I know you and the heavenly host of angels are amused when I am having one of those grandiose pity parties.

Love, peace, and joy,

Della Faye

CONTENTS

INTRODUCTION

The title of this book was inspired by Thomas A. Edison's quotation "Our greatest weakness lies in giving up. The most certain way to succeed is to *always try just one more time*."

During my teenage years, this thing called love struck me. My high school sweetheart told me he loved me and since we were so much in love, it was okay to have an intimate relationship. By the time I graduated from high school, I was the mother of three children. I will never forget the gasp of disbelief from my classmates on graduation day as they called my name and I walked across the stage and accepted my diploma. People were whispering, "How in the world did she do it [graduate on-time]?"

My belief in a power greater than myself, assistance from my family, and encouragement from my parents and teachers to *try just one more time* helped me achieve this goal. Embracing the principle of perseverance early in life has helped me throughout my life.

I am a believer in the Word and Power of Almighty God. It is necessary for us to believe if we are to receive and achieve in life. Thomas A. Edison never gave up on his goals and dreams; that is why he had many inventions. If our goals are to manifest, we must never become so discouraged that we give up. We must *always try just one more time.*

All goals are not material; some are spiritual, such as learning to forgive, loving others unconditionally, overcoming jealousy, overcoming fear, and dealing with anger, just to name a few. Nothing is impossible when we have conviction of the heart. God honors our faith. To the degree that we believe, and keep taking action toward achieving our goal, we will receive.

When we feel strongly about an idea or invention, we should perform a task each day to make our ideas a reality. If you believe strongly in your dream, then others can believe with you. If you doubt, then others will doubt as well. I believe that we are the source of the conditions manifested in our life.

If we become exasperated, we must do something that will give us a dose of encouragement. We will have to do this on a daily basis, just like taking our nutrition. Many individuals went to their grave without having a chance to say, "I'm sorry, please forgive me," or "I forgive you," or "I love you."

There are countless stories of individuals who were turned away from publishers, bankers, investors, producers, and companies that told them their story, their idea, their invention, their voice, or their product was not good enough. The turning point for the individuals who made their dream a reality was they didn't give up, but they *always tried one more time.*

Della Faye

1

Prayer and Meditation Changes Conditions

Have you talked to God lately? Do you ever withdraw to a solitary place and talk to God? I heard a beautiful quotation that says "Man's problems stem from his inability to sit alone in the silence."

When you are troubled and facing difficult times and decisions in your life, what do you do? Do you listen to the radio or TV? Do you consult family members or friends for advice? Do you read or busy yourself in work? Do you eat? Do you throw tantrums? Do you have your own pity party?

If you do any of these things, it's no fault of your own. From the time we were babies, our parents and guardians gave us toys and books, played or sang music to us, and turned on TV cartoons to soothe our fears and bouts of anguish. As we grew older, we found our own instruments and tools to soothe ourselves. We buy computers, boats, airplanes, and other such things to help us overcome our anguish.

Our parents raised us to the tune of distractions that are merely forms of numbing out and not dealing with hurtful or unpleasant situations. And we can all agree that the music, TV, video games, and other things only offer temporary fixes, temporary distractions.

How then do we get lasting peace? How do we get inner peace? How do we keep the faith in spite of the trials and tribulations? *Have you talked to God lately?* If we would withdraw from the noisy confusion of life and develop a dialogue with God, we would no doubt develop inner peace. Prayer is a dialogue between two persons who love each other.

When you go to God in prayer, are you specific in telling God what you want? Do you even know what you really want? Do you remember what you asked for after you pray? I'm sure you have heard the phrase *"be careful what you ask for, you might just get it."* I have often wondered how many people really believe they will receive exactly what they pray and ask for.

It reminds me of my prayer to God before I moved to Texas. I was a single mother with three boys. I prayed for God to bless us with a house with a washer, dryer, and a backyard. I no longer wanted to live in an apartment, but wanted my sons to experience life the way I grew up, in a house with a backyard to play in.

When I started searching for a place to live, I found myself looking at apartments instead of houses. I became very frustrated in my search when several rental agents turned me down, because the criterion was each child must have his own bedroom. Now, this was not feasible because all the complexes I visited had only three bedroom apartments.

It got to the point where I went home after visiting two or three complexes one day, got down on my knees and began weeping and having a serious pity party. I told

God that he didn't love me, because after all I had prayed about moving to Texas, and He had opened the doors and made the move possible. I mean I was really crying, doubting God's love for me, and thinking that I had made the wrong decision moving to Texas. Well, all of a sudden, a voice within said, *Della, what type of living quarters did you pray for before moving to Texas?*

I jumped up from my knees, stopped my pity party and crying, and instead began to give praise and thanksgiving to God for reminding me of what I had prayed and asked for. In less than two hours of giving praise and thanksgiving, my eldest sister called. She worked in housing at the University of Texas at Arlington. Our conversation went something like this: "Della, are you interested in looking at a house here in Arlington? I sent a lady to look at a house, and she came back and said the house was too big for her." My response: "Yes, of course I am interested. Where do I go or who do I call?" She gave the owner's telephone number to me, and I called. The owner said she lived two doors from the rental property, and I could come over immediately.

When I got to the house, the first things I noticed were the washing machine, dryer, huge kitchen, and the big side and back yards. I couldn't believe my eyes. It was a four-bedroom house; that meant each son would have his own bedroom. I got exactly what I had prayed for and some additional things such as the big side yard and huge kitchen. You see, I prayed for one thing but obviously did not believe God or did not think I was worthy enough to deserve what I prayed for.

If you are not receiving what you pray for, dear friend, search your own soul. Do you have confidence in God? Do you trust God? We must learn to talk with God instead of numbing out. When we talk with God, conditions will change in our life. Exactly what is it that you want or need? Bring your requests to God, then watch, wait, and cooperate. Tell Him in your prayer exactly what you need. Then have the faith and confidence that He will provide exactly what you asked for.

I am not saying that we can tell God what to do; we must come with a surrendered attitude as Jesus came. Sometimes our prayers will be for strength to endure trials, tribulations, and suffering. God knows what is best, and only God can see the end results. There will be times in our life when we pray, and it seems as though our prayers are going unanswered. If we have been clear about what we want, then we must leave our prayer at the altar and offer praise and thanksgiving. After all, what else can we do? Whatever the result, we cannot change it. Some things are just destined to happen. When we've done all we are supposed to do—prayed, maintained our faith, confessed our faults, loved others unconditionally, forgiven others for their sins, and lived the life that Christ and the great saints have taught us to live—the only thing left for us to do is leave our request at the altar, and go about our day offering praise and thanksgiving to God.

Have you talked to God lately, or do you seek the advice of others? Are your prayers going unanswered? Prayer is when we speak to God. Prayer is when we make our petitions and requests known.

If our prayers are going unanswered, maybe we need to sit alone in the silence and meditate. Meditation is when we allow God to speak to us. I said *when we allow God to speak to us*, because He does not force us to become still and know that He is God, always willing and wanting to guide our steps. Is there someone you need to forgive, or some changes you need to make in your own behavior?

What are you giving to the world? Take a good look at your life. Are you doing to others what you would have them do to you? *Blessed people bring blessings to everyone they meet.* We are the source of the conditions manifested in our lives. If we want love, then we must be a source of love. If we want peace, then we must be a source of peace. If we want forgiveness, then we too must forgive others.

If we want our prayers answered, we must live as Christ taught us to live. Are you selfish, stingy, or begrudging? Are you unforgiving? Are you judgmental? Do you just grumble and complain, or are you making a difference in the world? Are you helping to improve the quality of life, beginning with your own life? Yes, I know that you have endured suffering, trials, and tribulations, but the pity party must end some day if you want to make our world a better place.

God is a loving Father. He knows what we need and has provided us with everything to meet our needs. Do you take the initiative to do something good in others' lives, or are you busy waiting for the world to pay you homage?

What good and merciful actions have you performed lately? What attitude did you put on this morning? Did you look at all the good in your life and offer a prayer of thanksgiving, or did you wake up grumbling and complaining?

Whatever state and condition you find yourself in today, ask, "What is my lesson in this? What purpose does it serve in my life?" *Have you talked to God lately*? Have you confessed your faults? Have you prayed for others? Have you stopped grumbling and complaining? Have you asked God to reveal His purpose for your life? Have you asked, "What can I do to serve my fellowman? What can I do to make the world a better place?"

If you are unemployed, have you thought about volunteering your services? This is the advice my grandmother provided to us when we were still young. She would say, "If you cannot find a job, then go and volunteer your services; you never know who you will meet and how God will bless you while you are serving others."

When we learn to give, the universe will give to us. I once met a lady who told me, "You should keep the universe indebted to you, instead of you always being indebted to the universe." If the blessings are not overflowing in your life, just maybe you are indebted to the universe. Instead of always having the palm of your hand stretched out and facing upward, learn to place your palm face down—give to others.

Reach out and touch someone's hand; make this world a better place because you can. If we don't like the conditions manifested in our lives, we must change what we are creating each day. We make the sandwiches, we cook the meals, and we plant the seeds. We plant our seeds morning, noon, and night. God has provided the guidelines and instructions for living, yet we continue to make sandwiches that we don't like. Then we want to grumble and complain, blame our spouse, blame our kids, blame our boss, blame anybody but ourselves for the conditions manifested.

If you are tired, then it is time to stop doing things the same old way if you want different results. *Galatians 6:7* says, "whatsoever a man soweth, that shall he also reap." The law of compensation is: *Whatever we plant now, we will harvest later. Nothing can come from a human being but another human being; nothing will come from a monkey but a monkey. Therefore, it stands to reason that nothing will come from negativity, hatred, fear, grumbling, and complaining but more of the same.*

Have you talked to God lately? Are you still miserable, unhappy, and feel that your prayers are going unanswered? If you are, then it is time to follow Christ's example; find a solitary place, and pray to God. Once you pray, be willing to follow His advice. If you have done all that you are supposed to do, then stand firm, have faith, and believe.

2

Faith Brings the Desired Results

To have all our dreams come true, we must have a feeling that what we want will happen. We must have hope, and expect the desires of our heart to manifest. *Merriam-Webster's* dictionary defines *substance* as "the real or essential part of anything." It defines *hope* as "a feeling that what is wanted will happen." It also says that hope is "a desire accompanied by expectation," and that to hope means "to want and to expect."

I suppose it is really wise to expect what we want. To have all our dreams come true, we must have the faith of a little child. *A child's faith is perfect. A child accepts things at face value. They believe the promises and words spoken to them.* We also, referring to adults, must accept, believe, and have hope.

We must first see clearly in our minds the things we desire. We cannot see our minds, yet we know we have them. We cannot see spirit, yet spirit is real. We cannot see the wind, yet we know that it's there. Fear is our only enemy. *Nothing outside of us causes our lack of fulfillment or problems.* When we understand that we are the makers of the conditions manifested in our lives and the world, then we can change them.

To have all our dreams come true, we must build our desires in our inner world. Everything is first an idea. An idea is not an idea until it is acted upon. Every morning we should dedicate 15 to 30 minutes to create a clear and distinct mental picture of the things we have hoped for but not seen in our lives and the world.

We will have to reform our ideas, because reform begins at cause, and cause is mind. If we all start meditating, praying, and believing, I believe we will see different conditions manifested in the world. A transformation must occur if we want different results in our lives and in the world. Most of us are fearful of change. But when our attitude, thoughts, and disposition remain the same, why do we expect different results?

How can we measure our faith—by the conditions that continually manifest in our life? When we constantly pray to God and think that he is not responding, it is time to look at ourselves. Ask the question, "What am I doing or not doing?"

Our problems stem from our daily focus. When we look at what is, instead of what we want to see manifested, conditions remain the same. If we keep our focus on appearances, we will never believe God's promises. If our desires are to manifest, we must believe.

Faith requires work on our part. The work required is mental, and the result is a renewed mind. We must create mental pictures of things hoped for. What we plant now we will harvest later.

Faith does not require us to have a college degree to receive the things hoped for; we need only to believe. It doesn't matter if we have learning disabilities or never finished school; faith requires belief and trust in Almighty God.

Our faith must be applied. Whatever you're hoping for, you must take action and go after it. Let's say you are hoping for a new home. Find or take a picture of the home you want. Place the picture in several areas of your present living environment. Daily thank God for bringing the home you desire into your life.

When my family was looking for and found the home we wanted to purchase, I took the graphic [listing] sheet that describes everything about the house, such as the room size and number of rooms, and taped the words *SOLD TO THE SOWUNMI FAMILY* across the FOR SALE sign on the listing sheet. I typed the words in Microsoft PowerPoint, cut them out, and pasted them on the listing sheet. I then hung the listing sheet over the vanity in our bathroom as a daily reminder to thank God.

If a vacation is the thing hoped for, get all the pictures and literature you can find about the place you want to visit. Read everything about the desired vacation spot, and visualize that you are already there enjoying the vacation. If peace is the thing hoped for, then daily go within [meditate] and develop inner peace.

Everything we see and use was first a thought, a dream, or a vision in someone's mind. The clothing we wear, the cars we drive, the houses we live in, the chair you're sitting on were all someone's dream. These people had a dream or vision, and allowed nothing, and no one, to stop them from realizing their goals and dreams:

o   John F. Kennedy had a dream of us going to the moon.

o   Thomas Edison probably said, "I am tired of living in the dark; I want some light."

o   Rosa Parks was tired; she must have dreamed of equality for all. She decided, "*I am not moving to the back of the bus.*"

These people were ordinary people just like you and me. Yet now, they, along with the many other dreamers and visionaries, belong in a *Dreamers' Hall of Fame*. You might not live to see your dream manifest, but don't allow that to stop you from working toward it.

Your dream may be of a personal nature, such as to lose weight, to quit smoking, to stop grumbling and complaining, to purchase a new car, or to get out of debt and start saving money. The only way we will receive the things hoped for is by having faith that they will manifest in our lives. When we truly believe, nothing is impossible; the things hoped for will manifest. *Mark 9:23* tells us, ". . .All things are possible to him who believeth."

God wants us to prosper and be in health. He has already done His part. He has supplied everything that we need and provided a blueprint for how to acquire what we want and need. Repeat affirmations and verses daily when you wake up and before retiring each night.

Repeat affirmations throughout the day whenever the need arises. We live in a negative society; that should be reason enough for those who love the Lord not to contribute to the negativity. As we change internally, outer conditions will change.   Do not contribute to anyone's pity party; give them hope instead. Do not agree with their negativity; instead, teach them to apply God's truth and to believe in Almighty God.

Remember that we can repeat verbal prayers and say that we have faith, but until we apply the truth to each situation our conditions cannot change. *Hope is desire accompanied by expectation.* Teach others to expect the best from God, to expect goodness.   Do not look at outward appearances; keep your eyes and mind focused on what is expected.

Faith requires mental work and believing in the invisible. Faith requires total trust and reliance upon God. Faith also means closing our eyes and believing the impossible. I recall when my sister Linda wanted a new car. I advised her to be specific in the make, model, year, and color car she wanted. I encouraged her to write an affirmation and thank God in advance for the car she desired. She wrote the affirmation, hung it inside her closet door as a daily reminder to thank God, and within three months she had purchased the car.

I read that *the subconscious mind does not reason, reject, nor condemn; it merely seeks to accomplish what is impressed upon the heart, whether negative or positive.* You may not desire negative conditions, but if your mind is constantly focused on negativity and unpleasant conditions in your life, the law of compensation will bring to you the negative thoughts and things in your heart and mind. Change your thoughts, change the mental images you are creating, and the things you are hoping for can manifest.

A lack of faith could stem from a belief that you are being punished for some former action or sin. Evil and sin are not causes; they are results. God created us, but we make and mold ourselves by our thoughts. The *Bible* contains many stories and parables of the results achieved by those who had faith and believed in God. Take your time and read the entire 11th chapter of *Hebrews* to increase your faith. After reading the chapter, study the stories of each character mentioned.

Faith means we will have to believe without proof of certainty. It means standing on God's promises in spite of current conditions. Faith means affirming that the spirit of God within us inspires and guides us.

Faith means we must have hope, and hope is a feeling that what is wanted will happen. Hope is desire accompanied by expectation. Desire times expectation equals motivation.

If conditions in your life are not to your satisfaction or expectation, turn your attention and focus to the things hoped for. Build your desires in your inner world. Resolve to have unquestioning faith because it brings results. Outward appearances are illusions. Substance is the real part of everything.

Faith requires mental work, which means that we can do this work anywhere and anytime. We can create mental images while driving. We can recite and affirm biblical truths. We can do these exercises while cooking, exercising, gardening, mowing the lawn, working on the car, cleaning, or taking care of the children.

Who and what can stop you from putting faith to work in your life? Nobody but you. *Hebrews 11:6* says, "But without faith it is impossible to please him: for he that cometh to God must believe that he is, and that he is a rewarder of them that diligently seek him." You should also know that it also means without faith it is impossible to please yourself.

What things do you desire today? If you will only remember *Hebrews 11:1:* "Now faith is the substance of things hoped for, the evidence of things not seen." *Hope brings things to pass, because hope is a feeling that what is wanted will happen.*

What are those thoughts you are thinking? What words are you speaking? What actions are you taking? You are building those things within your world. Nothing outside of us causes our problems or lack of fulfillment. *We are the builders of that which is invisible, though it will become visible someday. It will manifest as prosperity or poverty. It will manifest as health or sickness. It will manifest as happiness or depression. It will manifest as joy or sorrow. It will manifest as love or fear. It will manifest as success or failure.*

3

Where There Is Fear There Is Not Enough Love

Since we were babies, we heard words and phrases such as *no, don't touch, stop,* and *quit.* It is from some of these statements that our fears were born. At that time in our lives, our parents were protecting us from some things that could harm us. *They had our backs; they had us covered, and that was good at the time.*

There's One today who has our backs, One who has us covered: He is God. If we will only allow Him to lead and guide us, we will not allow fear to stop us from achieving our purpose in life. *Where there is fear there is just not enough love.* Love is the total absence of fear.

We will never enjoy today if we fear tomorrow. There is a universal law, the *Law of Cause and Effect*. The causes of the conditions manifested in our lives and the world are a direct result of our own thoughts, words, and actions.

If what we have been thinking and doing is not working, it is time to redirect our energy in all we think and do. Think about this for a moment: If after nine months, your dad rushed your mom to the hospital for the big moment, the nurses prepared the room, the doctor showed up to deliver you, and out came a baby bird, a monkey, a tiger, or dog, there is no doubt there would have been a major uproar in the hospital.

But let us thank God for the perfect order in His universe. Let us thank God for the law of compensation, the *Law of Cause and Effect*. Nothing can come from a human being but another human being.

We are in control of our thoughts, and if we change our thoughts we will change the conditions manifested in our life. No one can get in our mind and make us feel fear, worry, or doubt.

There's a great book I recommend that you purchase, read, and reread. The title is *Hinds' Feet on High Places* by Hannah Hurnard. The book "is a beautiful allegory dramatizing the journey each of us must take before we can live in the high places." The book has some very interesting characters, such as the main character named Much-Afraid, and other family members named Bitterness, Self-Pity, Brother Craven Fear, Sister Spiteful, and Aunt Dismal Forebodings, just to name a few. The story is based on the scripture *Habakkuk 3:19*, "The Lord God is my strength, and he will make my feet like hinds' feet, and he will make me to walk upon mine high places."

Like the main character in *Hinds' Feet on High Places*, if we allow God to guide us, we can gain confidence and begin to experience love and overcome our fears. Is there a goal, aspiration, or mission in your life that you want to accomplish, but fear is holding you back? Is there someone in your life that you want to forgive, someone that is causing you anger, and what you feel is holding you back? If so, it is time to affirm the truth to receive and accomplish what God has in store for your life.

Continual application of truth causes the desired results.   Devote your attention to what you want manifested in your life instead of what you don't want. As you go through life, learn to live and enjoy each moment.

I want to suggest a key to overcoming fear: first, prayer and belief in God. Second, I recommend that you write an affirmation. The affirmation should affirm the type of person you want to present to the world. For an affirmation to be effective, write it in present tense form, such as *I am a powerful, caring, courageous leader,* or *I am a loving, devoted, and compassionate woman.* Do not allow anyone or anything to hold you back. Especially do not allow you to hold you back. Keep your eyes and mind focused on what you want to achieve in life. Don't be afraid to fail. When you make mistakes during life, don't give up; brush yourself off, and know that as stated in the famous poem *FOOTPRINTS,* God is carrying us when we least expect it.

If we suffer in this world, it is not because God has forgotten us but because we have forgotten to include God. And, even with God by our side, we are going to make mistakes; we are going to slip and fall, hurt and suffer. The rough spots are easier to bear when we know

God is by our side. *Throw off the hazard of being afraid to fail.* Are you afraid of being crucified at 33 like Jesus, being murdered like Martin Luther King, Jr., John F. Kennedy, or other great leaders? If so, what is the worst thing that could happen? Our family and friends would miss us, but we'll go to be with our Father.

Death: This is one great fear of many people. I once read a quotation that said, "Everyone wants to go to Heaven, but no one wants to die." I believe people are afraid of death because that is the final defeat to the ego, the ultimate loss of control. Pray, meditate, and trust God to lead you on your journey to accomplish your mission in life.

What happens is, we create comfort zones for ourselves, box ourselves in until we have no peace in our life or the world, because we are afraid of stepping outside the boundaries we have set for ourselves. What would happen to the world if people did not take risks, were afraid to experiment, if they failed and did not pick up the pieces to start over again? Do you think we would still be in the dark if Thomas Edison and others had decided to stop after they did not succeed the first time? Do you think there would not be airplanes if the Wright brothers had thrown in the towel?

What fear are you facing today? As Susan Jeffries suggests, we must *Feel the Fear and Do It Anyway*. Are you a person who gives up after the first attempt? I read that Colonel Sanders at the age of 65, used his $105 Social Security check to start his business; that Babe Ruth hit 714 home runs, but he also struck out 1,330 times? We, too, are going to strike out sometimes. We are going to make the wrong choices sometimes. If we will only persevere, we'll come out on top. We must keep company with people who motivate us, but most of all we must encourage and motivate ourselves. From time to time raise your hand over your shoulder and give yourself a pat on the back. Look into the mirror and tell yourself just how wonderful you are. We really are wonderful in spite of our past failures.

If what we tried failed, we are not a failure. Our failures are not to hold us back, but to make us a better person in the world, to refine us. Don't throw in the towel after failures. Ross Perot said, "Most people give up when they are about to achieve success. They quit on the one-yard line. They give up at the last minute of the game, one foot from a winning touchdown."

Here's a poem I wrote. I believe God sends this message to us. The title is *"Remember Me!"* "Remember me; I am the sunlight that shines brightly when you need sunshine to brighten your day. I am the voice in the wind that says, 'be still my dear trust in me and do not fear.' I am the raindrop that cleanses your soul and wash away all your tears. I am the moonlight that guides you during the darkest moments of your life. I am the air, the breath of life that you breathe eternally. May your fears dissipate and your dreams come true as you Remember Me!"

Yes we are always going to make mistakes, and experience trials and tribulations, but always remember *no condition is permanent in your life*.

4

No Condition is Permanent

We can listen to people and look at people, and their disposition will tell us a lot about them, whether they are happy or sad, friendly or not so friendly, enjoying life or struggling with life.

Are you, dear friend, facing obstacles in your life? Are you worried about your health and benefits? Are you unhappy in your love life? Are you worried about money troubles, debts or your work? Are there family troubles of any kind? Do war and violence upset you? If you are experiencing any of these problems, you must believe that *no condition is permanent*. We all face obstacles and experience trials and tribulations. Yet our instruction books for living provide answers and solutions.

Some problems and obstacles stem from our own thoughts and actions. Others are part of the divine plan; I believe they are to help us grow and become disciples for God. As we grow closer to God, we will experience trials and tribulations. But the *good news* is that *no condition is permanent*.

Throughout the *Bible* we find stories and history related to every obstacle and problem we face today. We all experience pleasant and unpleasant conditions in our lives. However, if we do our part the reward will be great.

I have prayed and asked myself countless times why God does not put an end to certain conditions and circumstances. If you have studied the *Bible* and come to know God, you know that He can stop anything at any time. Now, this being true, why do certain conditions in our lives and the world continually manifest? Why? Why? Why? I believe to allow spiritual maturity and to draw us closer to God and each other.

There is not one problem we face that God cannot solve. There is no uncertainty for which God does not have the answer. Life is full of change. Our struggles come when we are disobedient, afraid to step out of our comfort zone, and afraid to change.

We experience change in the universe constantly. Seconds turn into minutes, minutes into hours. Day turns to night. Spring turns to summer, summer to fall, and fall to winter. We experience rain, yet we also experience sunshine. The rain does not last forever. Learn to look for more rainbows in your life.

Our problems stem from our inability to change the CD tune we are playing repeatedly in our thoughts. When we experience unpleasant conditions, rather than take the condition to God in prayer, we play the negative tune over and over in our mind. Instead of focusing on what we want, we focus on what is.

The *Bible* says prayer and faith in God, not worry and doubt, is the solution to the problem. In other words, *no condition is permanent*. In other words, "walk by faith not by sight." No condition or obstacle is too big for God. What is required on our part is faith and obedience. We should not judge by outward appearances. We must have faith and believe.

Read the story of the walls of Jericho in the book of *Joshua*. From this story we should learn these things: (1) listening is required, (2) obedience is required, (3) no walls [conditions] are permanent, and (4) nothing can prevail against the Lord.

Do you listen to God's instructions and faithfully follow His guidance and leadership? Do you understand the importance of prerequisites or mandatory steps? First, an act or a certain attitude might be required of us. When you study the *Bible,* pay close attention to the word *"then,"* and, if some action or attitude is required on your part, you must surrender and obey—that is if you want the desired result to manifest in your life.

If we struggle in this world, it is because we have forgotten God, not that God has forgotten us. God loves every one of us. Divine love is the answer to the questions of our heart. I spend a lot of time studying and listening to inspirational books and tapes. The *Bible* contains the solutions and answers to our problems. However, we must learn to apply the truth to our lives; then we will have victory.

In the late seventies I was diagnosed with Rheumatoid Arthritis for which there is supposedly no cure. My doctors prescribed a variety of pills and cortisone shots to treat my condition. I couldn't understand or believe that I was experiencing such a diagnosis at such a young age; I was in my twenties. I refused to accept and believe that I would have to live with the condition for the rest of my life. I recall studying and reading to learn more about the disease. I also sought the prayers of many ministers and studied many different faiths. I cannot recall exactly when the pain subsided, but I remember trashing the bag of pills, and then no longer taking the shots.

Whenever I am experiencing unpleasant conditions, I always pray, meditate, and then play a song or read a favorite book or scripture that speaks to my heart. I will play a song over and over again until I achieve the desired results.

The real problems continue when we blame everything and everyone outside of us for the conditions that continually manifest. We walk around in denial. The problem could be because there is not enough self-love. If you are diagnosed with any condition, do you prepare to live, or do you prepare to die?

Don't be mad at friends and family members, coworkers, bosses, or anyone else if conditions in your life are not as you want them to be. What are you decreeing today by your own words? What are you visualizing today by your own thoughts? Are you part of the problem, or do you bring solutions? Are you making a difference in the world? As Shakespeare said, "This above all: to thine own self be true."

5

Against All Odds

"The odds are against you." This is a defeatist attitude statement. With attitudes and statements such as these, I am not surprised that many people live defeated lives. Whenever people tell me that the odds are against me, I am encouraged even more to find ways to overcome the odds and prove that it can be done. "It ain't over until the fat lady sings." This is a famous and often-recited quotation people use whenever there is a competition, great feat to accomplish, or major obstacle to overcome.

My friend Alice wanted to change careers, and she applied for a position in the local office of a nationwide company. She was informed that there were no current openings at the local office, and there probably wouldn't be for some time, because most staff members worked until retirement age. Alice decided to apply for a position in the corporate office, located in another state, and she was hired.

It was obvious that Alice never planned to leave her community for good because she never changed her driver's license, car tag, or bank account. She moved to the new community, but stayed focused on her main objective: obtaining a position at the office in her town. Alice never once thought that the odds were against her. She knew that with faith, prayer, belief in God, and her willingness to *try one more time,* that it truly wasn't over until the fat lady sang.

Since Alice never lost sight of her objective, within two years of working in the corporate office a position became available in the office located in her town. Well, of course she applied and received the position. Alice never allowed anyone to decide that the odds were against her, and, nine years later, she is still employed in the local office.

And what about those long distance love affairs? If someone tells you that they are in a long distance relationship, they will probably follow-up with the statement, *"I know you believe, like most people, they do not work."* My good friend, Erica, a devout Christian, came to me and shared how she had prayed and asked God for a mate. She met Maceo through some of her friends. However, Maceo lived in another state and she was constantly in fear, or shall I say suspicious, of him because of the distance between them. Maceo's work required constant contact with other females because of the nature of the business he was in. Deep inside, Erica felt that he could cheat on her and couldn't believe that he would be faithful to someone so many miles away. I remember asking her the reason she did not give God credit for sending the person that she had prayed for. I told Erica that is a major problem with most human beings: we pray and ask God for something in particular, yet do not trust God to bring the thing to pass. I reminded Erica that the odds were against her only if she believed they were. On the other hand, she could overcome her fears and believe the relationship would work even though it was a long-distance affair.

I recommended that she pray and write an affirmation to overcome her distrust. She began writing an affirmation, and before long they were engaged. Even when the odds are against us, we do not have to buy in to old fashioned and often outdated beliefs. Erica moved closer to Maceo, and in 1996 they got married.

To *try one more time* requires PMA, a *Positive Mental Attitude*. My sister, Pumpkin [her nickname], learned this and built her character around her beliefs. She did not allow the fact that she dropped out of high school to deter her from the education she decided to pursue later in life. She began by passing her General Education Development ("GED") tests and then later acquiring an Associate's Degree in Early Childhood Development. During a recent conversation about what she is now up to, and wants to accomplish, she told me she wants to further her college education by specializing in a particular field. She was also recently appointed the director of a daycare facility.

It is amazing how taking an initial step can lead to even more steps. Taking baby steps increases our self-confidence and ability to take giant steps. When we realize that we are not alone on the journey, we feel an urging to *try one more time.*

Do you remember the lady in the *Bible* with the blood issue that lasted more than twelve years? My sister Nita [Anita] was scheduled for major heart surgery October 2003 and experienced a lot of anxiety the morning before her surgery. She wept and cried as though the end were drawing nigh. For most of us, the unknown and unexpected always cause nervous tension and fear. Her first surgery was not completely successful. Over the next eight months after the initial surgery, Nita had three additional major heart surgeries. In the recovery period after the second surgery, the doctor told our mom, "You have a very sick daughter." Her recovery was very questionable, and we all worried. We prayed even more and continually solicited prayers on her behalf. Did Nita or the lady with the issue of blood play negative tunes over and over in their minds that attributed to their health troubles? What changed the course of their eventual outcome, their faith? Was it the prayers, encouragement, and support from family members and friends? We will never know. But one thing is for certain—there's always a hidden hand guiding us through the muddle and mess of life.

There are questions that we often cannot answer, but it is important to pray for and encourage others during difficult times. *Matthew 9:22* reveals Christ's comments to the lady with the issue of blood: "thy faith hath made thee whole." Make a commitment to take time from your day and visit family members and friends in hospitals, nursing homes, or experiencing ill health at home. Encourage them to keep the faith, trust in God, and pray *one more time,* especially when the odds seem to be against them.

6

There is Power in our Thoughts, Words, and Actions

When I was a young girl, my father would encourage me to watch my mother when she was cooking. He often told me that if I wanted to learn to cook, I should take lessons from my mother. I used to watch her prepare many dishes, such as turkey and dressing, peach cobbler, bake cakes, and many other dishes without following a recipe. Although I used a recipe, sometimes the dish did not turn out like hers or the way I expected.

Have you ever prepared a cake and forgot to add the eggs or the sugar before baking? You probably had to throw it out and start over. Whenever we bake a dish and fail to add a certain ingredient, it is really too late to add the ingredient once we have baked the dish. The next time around may require setting all the ingredients in front of us before we begin the preparation. If we cook a dish on top of the stove and forget to add a spice or to add just enough of a particular ingredient, we can doctor our dish up by adding the ingredient.

Eat the right foods and engage in the right type and amount of exercise is the advice given by many physicians and nutrition experts. But the greatest physician and nutrition expert says it is not what goes into the body, but rather what comes out of the heart, that causes our problems and causes the conditions manifested in our lives. Read *Mark 7:1-23* in the *Bible*.

Dr. Frank Crane said, "Our best friends and our worst enemies are our thoughts. A thought can do us more good than a doctor or a banker or a faithful friend. It can also do us more harm than a brick."

Does that mean we are in control of our destiny, since no one has control over our thoughts, what is in our heart? No one can rob us of our peace. In fact, when we apply this spiritual principle we should always experience joy.

Always remember *there is power within us*. Ephesians 3:20 says, *"Now to Him who is able to do exceedingly abundantly above all that we ask or think, according to the power that works in us."* Sometimes during our journey in life we allow past failures and misfortunes to stop us from pursing our goals and dreams, and enjoying the benefits of excellent health, great relationships, prosperity, security and peace of mind.

We can do many things because of the power that works in us. We are secured against any infectious fatal delusion *"because greater is he that is in you than he that is in the world."* I John 4:4.

We can overcome any addiction, handicap, fear, hardship, and weapon formed against us. We can forgive any hurt. We can turn misfortune into an opportunity.

Every great athlete has a coach, someone who motivates, inspires, and encourages him/her. God sent Jesus Christ to teach us in the way that we could have victory in our life. Our problem is that we do not follow His recipe, the principles of which were handed down by God.

My favorite basketball player of all times, famous basketball star, Michael Jordan, and the Chicago Bulls took their talents onto the basketball court during the championship game in June 1998 against Carl Malone and the Utah Jazz. Their coaches, Phil and Jerry, sat on the side lines, observed their teams' actions, gave specific plays, and offered advice for their teams to win the championship game. Phil and Jerry were former players, and their purpose was to share plays that they thought would win the game. Each player had a certain talent and attitude that he brought to the game and the coaches' purpose was to provide the right mix and mixtures for 48 minutes. Who and what determined if the right mix was on the floor? The end result was the determining factor—Chicago defeated Utah. Can we say that Chicago added the right ingredients and the right mix during that championship game?

God has provided His Word for us to have victories in our life. The *Bible* tells us that God created the universe by the Words of His mouth. The phrase "and God said" appears ten times in the first chapter of *Genesis*.

We release our faith in our words. If we would grasp and understand this truth we would have more victories in our life. We would have the peace that we all desire. By our own words we can give to another the greatest happiness or cause utter despair. Yes, there is power in what we say and think. Do not hold yourself in bondage by your thoughts and the use of your words.

If we are functioning at only a fraction of our potential, generally it is not because of a lack of skill or knowledge, but because of our attitude or because we are being mentally run down by the comments and mental abuse from others, including family members. We must help others become self-leaders. We can help people improve by offering praise. If someone we know and love does something right, we should praise them—even if what was done is not perfect. There is too much hatred, war, and chaos among family members, coworkers, and others because of criticism and ridicule. We must look for and praise progress.

Instead of holding back information and criticizing others, learn to empower others with your words. When someone is learning how to do something new or different, give that person more information that will help him or her perform even better. Many human beings are living defeated lives because no one wants to encourage or empower them.

I read that Michael Jordan's school basketball coach told him in so many words that he was not ready for the high school varsity basketball team. Instead of being discouraged, Michael believed in his *natural talents* and went on to become one of the greatest players in basketball history.

Learn to improve yourself if you want to improve the world. Instead of speaking about conditions as they appear, learn to speak the desired results. Do not continually speak the problem, for if you do you keep it bound and tied to you.

How do we master talents that do not come naturally? Practice, practice, and practice! Write and use affirmations until you get them deep down in your heart. Pray for a transformation to occur in your life. You must be willing to have something different occur in your life. Be willing to surrender old worn out habit patterns. If we sincerely want to experience different results in our life, prayer, meditation, faith, studying the Bible, and reading other motivational literature, being careful of the words that we speak—planting good seeds with our words to ensure a blessed harvest, removing the weeds as they begin to sprout, setting goals, writing them down and taking action by working to achieve them, rejoicing more often, and giving thanks more often, purposely doing something different, and a strong belief in God, along with action on our part, will bring about different conditions.

Adopt the attitude *if it is to be, it begins with me.* If you know that the ingredients [elements] within you are causing you and those around you to suffer, yet you refuse to change, do you really want different conditions in your life? Whenever necessary, apply Jesus' words and say to your own evil thoughts and words, "Get thee behind me, Satan."

Yes, every great athlete has a coach, and we can all learn from the wisdom of great leaders that have gone on before us.

Martin Luther King, Jr. said, "All men are caught in an escapable network of mutuality, tied to a single garment of destiny. Whatever affects one directly affects all indirectly—you can never be what you ought to be until I am what I ought to be."

7

What Will People Remember About You?

Many biblical principles teach us the cause and effect of the conditions manifested in our lives, thus in the world. The *Bible* teaches us to encourage one another. *What will people remember about you when you leave their presence? What will people remember most about you when you die?*

In everyday living we experience a variety of man-made laws. The traffic laws, money laws, work laws, moral laws, and many other laws that we abide by are for our own good. The laws are established to bring order where there might be confusion, peace where there is war and chaos, health where there is sickness and disease, and wealth where there is poverty.

Universal laws govern all living things, and all living things operate based on the laws. Plant an apple seed, and you will harvest apples. God created the universal laws to bring form to a world that was void and without purpose.

As human beings we sow our seeds morning, noon, and night. The seeds take form at some level. If the harvest you are reaping is full of weeds, then pull the weeds daily that are causing you or others pain.

To begin, you must know that there is nothing external that makes us happy. Our happiness comes from within. Whatever we build internally is manifested externally.

Will people remember you because of your love to others? Love means taking action to meet another person's needs. Are you like the Good Samaritan Jesus referred to in the *Bible*? Will people remember you as one who *loved your neighbor as yourself?*

Will people remember you as a peacemaker and forgiving person? One way to attain peace in our society is through every individual developing peace within his/her heart and soul. People will always respond in the manner we treat them. If you want peace in the world, then you must be a source for peace.

o   Dr. Wayne Dyer said, "Rather than be against war, be for peace."

Relinquish the need to be right and take a stand for peace.   Sometimes that will mean walking away from people and situations rather than fighting.   If a person does not have someone to fight externally, his or her war can only be internal.   They will transform their attitude and change internally.

I know that you have been hurt, as I have. I know that you don't think you can forgive your offender for the hurt, and that you feel you did not deserve the act or acts committed against you. But remember that Jesus did not do anything either.   In fact, in *Luke 23:34* Jesus said, "Father, forgive them; for they know not what they do."

When I moved to Texas, I prayed and asked God's blessing on my move.   As I was preparing to move, stumbling blocks appeared. I went to God again and said,

"I prayed and I thought you gave the green light, the go ahead to move, so why now am I experiencing these problems?"

Well, in two or three days after I prayed that prayer, I had a dream one night. In my dream, two ladies appeared that I had no association or respect for. The ladies lived in my community; we grew up together, and I knew they didn't like me. I adopted the same attitude. If they don't like me, then I don't like them. When we passed each other, we would not speak and would even roll our eyes at each other.

When I had that dream, I knew God was telling me, *"Della, you cannot move away from this place until you befriend these ladies."* Let me share the workings of God in our life. Within the next week or two I came across one lady in the grocery store. You better believe that I approached her and instantly started talking with her, as if we were the best of friends. She was very open and responsive to my communication.

I did not see the other lady before I moved. But, three years after I moved to Texas, I returned home to attend my sister's wedding. I went to the mall to shop and ran right into the other lady. Again, I instantly started a conversation with this lady, and she too was receptive and open to the communication.

The experience and dream taught me another lesson in life, and I always share this testimony with other people. If we continually pray and ask God for direction and reason behind the seemingly unpleasant situations and circumstances in our life, the reason that some of our prayers are going unanswered, He will always give us the answer, whether in a dream or through some biblical story, *Bible* verse, or parable. However, God leaves the rest to us. It is our choice to obey or disobey. If we choose to disobey we will continually go through the lessons.

I am not saying that we have to continually break bread, drink tea, or go to breakfast, lunch, or dinner with our offenders. I am saying that God asks us merely to forgive, not to pardon. We cannot pardon another. She/he must still stand before God. *Romans 12:19* says, "Dearly beloved, avenge not yourselves, but rather give place unto wrath: for it is written, Vengeance is mine; I will repay, saith the Lord."

We must leave justice for Heaven and treat the person the way we want to be treated. Forgiveness involves *our* attitude toward the person who hurt us. When we truly forgive, we are no longer hating the person or wishing ill fate upon him/her. On the contrary, we should want the best for him/her, which include repentance and restitution on their part toward God, others, and us.

How do we know when we have forgiven others? Are you killing their reputation and encouraging others to destroy them? Are you still thinking evil thoughts about them? It is time to discontinue worn out habit patterns, attitudes, and beliefs that no longer serve us. Our own resurrection will occur once we stop criticizing and belittling others, and when we let go of guilt, resentment, hatred, anger, and self-condemnation.

In addition to forgiving others, we must forgive ourselves. It is very important that we forgive ourselves for the things we have done and hold against ourselves. If we cannot forgive ourselves, then we'll have a difficult time forgiving others. Study the book of *Romans*. *Romans 8:1* says, "There is therefore now no condemnation to them which are in Christ Jesus, who walk not after the flesh, but after the Spirit."

Will people remember you because of your joy, including the joy you bring to others? The book of *Philippians* is considered the joy book of the *Bible*. The idea of rejoicing or joy appears sixteen times in the four chapters of this book. Do you want to experience more joy in your life? Then learn to treat others and yourself the way Christ treated people.

Will people remember you for your patience and understanding? We must try to understand others. We are never on the same path. It may take others some time to recognize the need for change in their life. Manipulation will not change people; only God can change someone's heart.

I am a person who likes to have her way, so when obstacles and problems arise I go to our Heavenly Father for the answer. Sometimes I think to myself, I must really amuse God and the heavenly angels. One day I angered a coworker to the point where she didn't want to talk with me anymore. Another coworker went to the lady and said, "I understand you are angry with Della." The lady's response: "Della will not let you be angry with her."

She is right. I have always been one to try to keep the peace. I would go to her desk every day, sometimes twice per day, to ask if she were still angry with me. She eventually gave in and forgave me. I suppose friendship and forgiveness were equally important to her. It's really a matter of allowing the Christ in us to see the Christ in others.

Will you be remembered for your kind and gentle words? Proverbs 15:1 – "A soft answer turns away wrath." We must remember that we are the mouth, hands, and feet for Christ. In every situation ask yourself the question, "What would Jesus do or say?" We must do our part to make a difference in the world.

Will people remember you because of your goodness? Henry David Thoreau said, "Goodness is the only investment that never fails." Do you apply goodness to your relationships with others? Can others depend on you? Are you an asset or a liability? Are you part of the wrecking crew or the construction crew? If honesty, kindness, and justice are not a part of your value system, redirect your energy.

Will people remember you as a humble servant? Will people remember you as a person who treated others with respect and common courtesy? Will you be remembered because of your sympathy toward others?

Will people remember you as a Diotrephes—one who is puffed up and proud in spirit, according to *3 John 1:9.*

We reap what we have sown. We are all affected by the conditions manifesting in the world because we all live together on earth. Our progress toward loving others requires a transformation of attitudes and values until our life eventually reflects the Christ. We are here to complement each other, not to compete with each other. We are here to love each other unconditionally.

We must replace unhealthy standards, whether through our thoughts, words, actions, music, TV programs, or books. We must start loving each other, instead of concerning ourselves with thoughts such as "people will think I care too much" or "this is not the place to show love." If we see a person in need of love, someone who needs someone just to listen, someone who needs someone to talk to, or someone who needs a hug because his/her spirit is wounded, whatever spot that person is in is the right spot to provide what they need.

Will people remember you for your compassion? What seeds are you sowing today? Experience and insight have taught me that bad crops affect all. All are affected by wars. Are you concerned about the conditions that are manifesting in our world? Are you concerned enough about the conditions in the world to devote time to different ministries that support prisons, missions, and city slums?

Will people remember you for transforming your attitude, value system, and for leaving the world in a better condition than you found it? One of the greatest contributors and inventors in the world, Thomas A. Edison, said, "Our greatest weakness lies in giving up. The most certain way to succeed is to *always try just one more time.*"

What one divine quality will people remember about you?

8

Hunches, Intuition, Premonitions, Telepathy

Everyone has had a premonition, hunch or telepathic thought about an event or person, and the thing came to pass and the persons crossed paths. How often have you thought about a friend who called, or you saw within a matter of days or weeks? Your friend or family member might even make the comment, "I was just thinking about you." If you entered the room, or called while people were commenting or making reference about you, Aunt Sister, as we called her, would say, "You are going to live a long time."

Would you agree that we could save ourselves a lot of anguish and frustration if we followed our intuition and listened to that voice within, the voice of God? I can recall many instances where I later commented *I should have followed my first mind.* Experience is a good teacher. As human beings, I think we learn best from the school of hard knocks; the lessons seem to have a lasting effect, and greater impact, than the subtle lessons. Do you find yourself trusting your intuition more as you grow older?

Being in tune with each other, especially those close to us, has benefits if we pay attention. We might save a life if we start caring more for each other. There would be less suicide if people made a call when they feel the strong urge, or stopped by to see a person who is constantly on their mind. I know because that is what changed my friend John's life. You see, he had given up hope when his wife decided that she no longer wanted to be married. That was okay, except she took all the family funds from the bank account, ran up a lot of debt before departing, and left John with all of this debt and no money in the bank.

In a matter of hours he lost hope. But, thank God, he had a couple of friends who paid attention to their hunches, the Christ within, and felt the urge to call him. Thank God we followed our intuition and called John because it literally was a matter of life and death. John later told us how we saved his life. He said he was sitting at the table with all the pills that he could find in the house. He didn't see any reason to live. He felt betrayed, let down, and rejected, and was contemplating suicide. He thought the best solution to his problem was to end it all. What was there to live for?

God had a plan for John. When I called John that evening, we invited him to come over to our house. As we sat chatting, we discovered what he was going through. On that day, I shared my own solution for dealing with problems that seem unbearable. I told him I find one of my favorite CD's, put it on the stereo, and play the tune that speaks to my heart [my problem] over and over again until I get the message deep down into my soul. Shirley Caesar's song *"He's Working It Out For You"* was the song I recommended.

I later discovered that John owned several of Shirley Caesar's albums, but never thought that playing a song over and over could change his attitude and soothe his anguish. He told me it had been four years since the event, and he had the opportunity to share his story with Shirley Caesar.

How many friends and family members would have been affected by his actions, and where would John be today had he not tried just one more time? Dear friend, I encourage you to *Always Try Just One More Time;* there really is light at the end of the tunnel.

9

Loving

I wish there were a class beginning with kindergarten that taught all the attributes of Love. I suppose educators feel that knowing how to love is the part of life that parents should teach through the *Bible* and by their own example. But if parents love us the way their parents loved and taught them, sometimes that love or lack of love can be very painful. The best teacher (or example) is a person who displays genuine love. We should study the attributes of this teacher and follow his/her example.

In *Romans 12:10* Paul says, "Be devoted to one another in brotherly love." I believe Paul is saying that God wants us to be imitators of him, because over in *Ephesians 5:1-2* he says, "Be imitators of God, therefore, as dearly loved children and live a life of Love, just as Christ loved us and gave himself up for us as a fragrant offering and sacrifice to God."

In life, *people don't care how much we know until they know how much we really care.* People cannot believe a message about love when their stomach is growling from hunger pangs. We must take action and not render lip service only. We are to express our love, and there are many ways we express love. One way we express love is by keeping our word (integrity.) When we are unable to keep our word, a telephone call to the person explaining our reason(s) for not keeping our word or to cancel an appointment is an expression of love as well as respect and courtesy.

Acceptance of people is another expression of love. Often we act as if we have arrived, that we have no vices, and that we are perfect human beings. But according to the *Bible not one of us is perfect.*

I met a man in the grocery store where I shopped each Sunday after church. He was one of the produce clerks. Every Sunday I would go to the grocery store near my church to buy fruit for the upcoming week. Bananas are one fruit I purchase every week. That Sunday, I was looking over the bananas trying to find a few ripe bananas to eat when I walked out of the store because I was hungry. A guy named Terry approached me. He had packaged several bags of very ripe bananas and said to me, "Why don't you purchase this bag of bananas, make some banana bread and invite me over for a piece?" It was something about the way he approached me. Obviously he was looking for a new friend and stopped what he was doing to get my attention. He got my attention all right. As he suggested, I purchased the bananas. He asked if we could trade telephone numbers. I agreed and listened to that still small voice. I acted according to *Colossians 3:14,* which says, "And above all things put on charity [love], which is the bond of perfectness." Later during the week I made the banana bread, called, and invited him to come and *break bread* with me.

Terry was very observant. When he came to my door, he had flowers, a box of peppermint candy, and a stuffed animal. He said he brought me flowers because *he noticed* I purchased flowers for myself the day I bought the bananas. He said the candy represented my sweet smile, and the stuffed animal was always to remind me of our friendship.

After that first date, several phone conversations, and trips to the movies, he came by my house one day with flowers, and this time he had a card in his hand. I want to share the message from the card with you. The front of the card says: "Friendship is a flower that blossoms in the heart." The inside was blank and he wrote this personal message: *"There comes a time in everyone's life when fate blesses you in a very special way. Della...that time has come for me. Meeting you has been such a blessing to my heart and my life. I now wake up each morning with a smile in my heart and on my face. What a wondering person you are! I am so thankful for your openness and your willingness to* <u>accept</u> *people as they are and* <u>not</u> *as you think they should be. I cannot predict what will become of our relationship, but I do hope it becomes something so special and so powerful that neither one of us will ever be able to walk away. Thank you for bringing joy, love, laughter, and above all . . .romance back in my life. I will always appreciate you for that."* He then signed the card Love Terry, *Matthew 6:33.*

Occasionally when I meditate, and reflect on life, I realize that one problem in the world today is a lot of people don't accept people as they are. So often we are busy trying to fix people, as if they are broken and in need of repairing. In fact, I know people, who turn their noses up to people if they do not have a certain type of job, do not drive a certain type of car, or live in a certain part of town, or have XX dollars in the bank. In 1992 when I told a friend how I met Terry, she told me there is no way she would date a man working as a produce clerk.

I married Terry within six months after our initial meeting. Now, that was unusual for me. In fact, my sister told me that our mother asked, "Who is this man Terry that Della is marrying; I have never really heard her talk much about him?" Terry and I met in Dallas and my family lives in Indiana and had not met him yet.

Right before I married him, I traveled to his hometown near Birmingham, Alabama. I discovered that he was an Evangelist, was involved in youth ministry, and had a good sum of money saved in the bank. Most of us would probably think that a produce clerk would not have any money saved, let alone the ten thousand plus dollars that he had saved. I guess that is the reason *Matthew 7:1* says, "Judge not, that ye be not judged."

Seven months into our marriage, Terry was diagnosed with non-Hodgkin's lymphoma, a form of cancer. Within one year of the diagnosis he expired. We dated and were married less than two years. That relationship has continued to affect the way I live my life. We never know who we are entertaining. And, if you don't believe in *love at first sight*, I encourage you to read *Genesis 24:52-67,* the story of Rebekah and Isaac.

Three months after Terry became ill, I was dressing for the 8:00 a.m. church service one Sunday. Terry decided that he didn't want to go that morning. His doctors told me that he could be mean and angry occasionally, and asked that I not take it personally. There were times when I did take it personally, human nature I suppose. When I entered the car that morning, I started crying and talking to God, telling him that I needed prayer, and did not want to attend our church because they did not have altar call at the 8:00 a.m. service. I thought to myself, if I were in Dallas or my hometown in Indiana, I could go to friends or prayer partners and ask them to pray with me. If I were in Indiana, I could drive to Lake Michigan and sit by the water and talk to God, and He could help me overcome the despair and distress I was feeling.

As I was crying out, I began speaking in a language unknown to me. In my despair, I drove toward our church even though I didn't want to go. This is the church Terry's family attended when he was growing up and where he was currently an associate minister. I reached the church between 8:10 and 8:15 a.m., walked in, and took my seat beside my mother-in-law. After sitting for what seemed like 2 or 3 minutes, the pastor said, "God has spoken to me and said that we need to have altar call this morning. I know that we never have altar call at the 8:00 a.m. service, but God said that we must today."

I jumped from my seat and probably was the first person at the altar. I cannot tell you what the pastor prayed that day because I was crying profusely and saying,

"God, you love me that much, you care that much about little bitty me, you care that much about your Della Faye, so much so that you went before me to the church, and told the pastor to have altar call."

Wow! What an eye opener for me. God really loves and cares for His children and listens to them. After altar call, I took my seat beside my mother-in-law, and she bent over and whispered in my ear, "I have been coming to this church and the 8:00 a.m. service for more than 20 years, and they never have altar call at this service. I saw you crying very hard. Did you give a note to the deacon or to the pastor to pray for you"? I said, "No, I did not, but God did."

After church I told my mother-in-law what I had experienced that morning while driving to church. She told me, "It scares me to love you as much as I do, and there's something about you that makes a difference in people's lives." I told her and I tell people even today, "It is not I, but the Christ in me. I didn't get this way overnight. I have my moments, as we all do. But prayer, faith, and obedience can change people, the same way that it changed me."

I was talking with a friend, and he told me that when he started dating his wife, there were problems in the relationship, things about each other that they did not like. The couple agreed to work on those areas. He said they took a blank sheet of paper and wrote down all the problems, being as honest and frank as possible. They wrote them down using a pencil with an eraser. As they worked on and eliminated each problem, they would erase it from the sheet.

Our problems could stem from a lack of self-love. If we don't love self, can we give love to someone else? Giving something away that we do not possess is hard. You may not be the person you want to be at this time. You may not like yourself, and others may not like the Being that you are presenting to the world, but prayer and God can change you. Develop new habits, new thought patterns, which lead to different choices and different actions. If we continue to love everyone no matter their present condition, love will take roots and grow in this world.

10

Serving

Everything in God's universe has a purpose. Yet, so often I hear people say, *"I don't know my purpose."* I believe all creation's purpose is to serve. If you are serving in any way, you are fulfilling a purpose. If you are not serving, then get busy. Go to the Lord and ask him to reveal His purpose for your life. It is never too late to begin.

A servant is the person who sees something that needs to be done and does not wait for someone to ask. This person takes the initiative and does it like a faithful servant. True leaders and servants appreciate other people's worth and realize that they are not above any job. True servants look for ways to serve better. And, there are many ways and many capacities in which we can serve and do presently serve.

As parents we serve our children.

As children we serve our parents.

As spouses we serve our significant others.

As employees we serve our employers.

As employers we serve our employees and clients.

As friends we serve our friends.

As loving, caring, compassionate human beings who care for the universe, including the plants, animals, lakes, and those people unable to care for themselves due to sickness, old age, or whatever the problem, we are serving God and fulfilling a purpose. Amazingly, we are not the only ones serving. I think our problem at times is that we feel as though we are serving, and that no one is serving us in return.

When God created the universe, He provided everything that we need including the faculties to create new and different things. And we should honor Him by taking care of that which He provided. Servants do not judge. Mother Teresa said, "If you judge people, you have no time to love them."

Servants give unconditional love and service. Servants are good listeners. Sometimes people need someone just to listen. I read a quotation that said, "We are not put on this earth for ourselves, but are placed here for each other. If you are there for others, then in time of need, someone will be there for you."

Think about it—someone serving, designed, engineered, manufactured, and carried across the highway the automobile you are driving. Many different servants planted, toiled, cared for, picked, cleaned, packaged, and delivered to market the food we eat. The clothes we wear were designed, cut, sewn, and delivered to the retailer; they were then unboxed, hung or folded by someone serving. Many different people also built the houses we live in.

Yes, everybody serves a purpose. What capacity are you serving in today? Are you serving with enthusiasm, joy, and gladness in your heart, or are you serving with anger, hatred, discontentment, or fear? Do you want to experience joy and happiness? Dr. Albert Schweitzer had this to say about really being happy: "I do not know what your destiny will be, but one thing I know: The only ones among you who will be really happy are those who will have sought and found how to serve."

If you do not have joy and peace in your heart right now in the capacity that you are serving, maybe you are not doing your life's work. And, how do we know when we are doing our lives' work? We know because we have joy and peace in our hearts. We get up and go about our day serving with glad hearts, with much love, compassion, and gratitude. We want to serve from sun-up to sundown. We find so much joy and peace when we are making a difference in this world.

Maybe you have not found your life's passion. If you do not like numbers, why work in a capacity that requires an aptitude for numbers? If you are working in customer service, yet do not enjoy meeting, greeting, and helping people, why work in this capacity? We do not serve society or ourselves well when we work in areas that cause us pain and suffering, that cause us to have a bad attitude.

Are you working in the capacity you are in because of your parents, your spouse, or your friends? Because your dad was a doctor does not mean that you should be a doctor. Because your brother is a lawyer is not reason enough for you to be a lawyer. You must become still, pray, meditate, and search your soul. God will inspire and guide you to your good, to His purpose for your life. God wants us to serve in those capacities that lift us up and lift others up as well.

Find your passion and begin to serve in that capacity. If you love cooking, then you should be the best chef in your area. If there is something that is troubling you, some fear, some negative or pessimistic attitude that is keeping you from your purpose, you must change it. You, and only you, have control over your own thoughts.

We must follow God's lead. Sometimes we may be puzzled and doubt what God asks us to do. Do you remember the biblical account in *Matthew 14:28-30* of Jesus walking on the water and inviting Peter to walk on the water with Him? It says, "And Peter answered him and said, 'Lord, if it be thou, bid me come unto thee on the water.' And he said, 'come.' And when Peter was come down out of the ship, he walked on the water, to go to Jesus. But when he saw the wind boisterous, he was afraid; and beginning to sink, he cried, saying, 'Lord, save me.'" Peter was okay until *he thought about what he was doing*. I can imagine him thinking: "Oh! My God, what am I doing? This is not solid ground." I believe he began to fear and look at things as they appeared, instead of what he was to achieve. And his thoughts caused the conditions that manifested in that moment. *Matthew 14:31-32* says, "And immediately Jesus stretched forth his hand, and caught him, and said unto him, 'O thou of little faith, wherefore didst thou doubt?' And when they were come into the ship, the wind ceased."

Everything begins internally: fear and doubt, or faith and trust. We must have faith and trust that God will not mislead, misdirect, or misguide us. It is when we think negative thoughts, speak negatively, and act according to our own plan that we experience discontentment. Charles Swindoll, in his book, *Growing Strong In The Seasons of Life* says, "God asks that we believe him regardless of the risks—in spite of the danger—ignoring the odds."

As you go through life, encourage someone and look for ways to serve. If you are unhappy or dissatisfied serving in your current capacity, become still by sitting alone in the silence, meditate, and say "God I surrender this day to you. What would you have me to do?"

11

Conclusion [Self-Discipline]

When I began writing this book, I was of the belief that perseverance was the real key to accomplishing goals, but I have since discovered that self-discipline is required to accomplish our goals. Even perseverance requires self-discipline. *Merriam-Webster* defines *self-discipline* as: *"correction or regulation of oneself for the sake of improvement."*

At this point in my life, all of a sudden I cannot drink coffee including the decaffeinated brands. Whenever I drink coffee, I experience stomach pain. Even though I experience pain, I still crave the flavor and taste of coffee. On several occasions, I allowed my cravings to overrule my senses and drank a cup of coffee, and within several minutes I experienced the stomach pain.

As I sit writing the conclusion for this book, I am craving coffee and have been almost tempted to make a pot and drink at least a cup to satisfy my cravings. I came to realize that the cravings are really just a pattern of behavior that I created since staying up late at night. Just five days ago I drank a cup of coffee and experienced severe stomach pain. At that time, I made a vow to change my behavior, probably the second or third promise to myself. Tonight it took discipline to change my mental faculties.

I remember going through the same *disciplinary* issues when I decided to quit smoking years ago. There were several instances when I had a desire to smoke, and almost gave in to the desire. I recall asking myself what payoff I expected from my behavior. This *self-talk* led to not smoking for the past 11 years.

Why do people give up? Why do we give in to our cravings and desires, even when we know they are harmful? Why do we give in if it is not leading to our ultimate goal and victory? The powerful, dominant, and controlling ego [conscious] that is resistant to change is what keeps us from changing our behavior. How do we acquire the discipline necessary for achieving our goals and experiencing the rewards—by accessing the subconscious—through prayer and meditation?

Remember, according to psychologists *the subconscious mind does not reason, reject, nor condemn; it merely sets out, seeking to accomplish that which is programmed into it;* the ego mind, conscious mind, which controls our thoughts and behavior, needs reprogramming. The way to reprogram and change our *pattern of behavior is through training*—through the subconscious mind.

Self-control is what we need, and the greater our self-control the greater our ability to achieve our goals. We have to deny ourselves some things in order to enjoy other things. It sure was nice when we had a parent, teacher, big brother and sister, or instructor to assist us in improving; they told us exactly what we had to do to get to the next level or step in life. They told us what changes were necessary. Now, the school of hard knocks [experiences], trials and tribulations, ups and downs, are our instructors and teachers. There's no passing to the next level until we learn the particular lesson before us.

The school of hard knocks doesn't care whether we repeat each lesson over and over again. This school has lots of time and space available. If we fail to comprehend, we'll just continually repeat the lessons.

Finally, we cannot stop the negative thoughts from coming, but we can surely replace the thoughts and eventually improve the behavior. The key questions for us are, *what is my payoff, what do I expect to accomplish, and what end-result do I want to achieve?*

There's a progress journal at the end of this book; use it and keep a journal of your progress. Pat yourself on the back from time-to-time. Reward yourself when you overcome any negative behavior pattern or accomplish even the smallest goal or task. I wish you a lot of success on your journey. Plant this phrase deep within your subconscious—I will *Always Try Just One More Time.*

REFERENCES

SOURCE	CHAPTER LOCATED
Merriam-Webster On-Line Dictionary	2
Hannah Hurnard, *Hinds' Feet on High Places* (American Edition Tyndale House © 1975)	3
Susan Jeffries, *Feel the Fear and Do It Anyway* (Ballatine Books, © 1988)	3
Colonel Sanders (www.KFC.Com)	3
Babe Ruth (www.baseballreference.com)	3
H. Ross Perot (www.brainyquote.com/quotes)	3
Dr. Wayne Dyer, *Staying on the Path* (Hay House, © 1995)	7
Shirley Caesar, *He's Working It Out For You* (Sony, Audio CD, Released: November 26, 1991)	8

Charles Swindoll, *Growing Strong in the Seasons of Life*
(Zondervan Publishing House © 1983)   10

SCRIPTURE INDEX

Romans
8:1	7
12:10	9
12:19	7

Galatians
6:7	1

Ephesians
5:1-2	9

Philippians 7

Colossians
3:14	9

Hebrews
11:1	2
11:6	2

3 John
1:9	7

MY PROGRESS JOURNAL

MY PROGRESS JOURNAL

MY PROGRESS JOURNAL

MY PROGRESS JOURNAL

MY PROGRESS JOURNAL

MY PROGRESS JOURNAL

MY PROGRESS JOURNAL

MY PROGRESS JOURNAL

MY PROGRESS JOURNAL